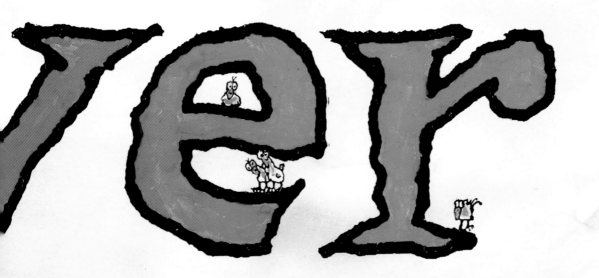

tease
a
weasel

by Jean Conder Soule

illustrations by George Booth

Random House 🏠 New York

You can knit a kitten mittens
And perhaps that cat would purr.

You could fit a fox with socks
That exactly matched his fur.

You could make a goat a coat
With a collar trimmed in mink;

Or give a pig a wig
In a dainty shade of pink.

But **never** tease a weasel;
This is very good advice.
A weasel will not like it —
And teasing
                isn't
                        nice!

You could make a riding habit
    For a rabbit if you choose;

PLOP

PLOPPITY

PLOP

PLOP

Or make a turkey perky
With a pair of high-heeled shoes.

You could make a collie jolly
With a red crocheted cravat;

Or make a possum blossom
In an Easter Sunday hat.

But **never** tease a weasel,
Not even once or twice.
A weasel will not like it —
And teasing
isn't
nice!

You could build a mouse a house
With a chimney made of bricks.

You could give a dove some gloves
And a set of walking sticks.

But **never** tease a weasel.
There! Now I've said it thrice.
A weasel will not like it—
And teasing
isn't
nice!

You could give a mule a pool
And some jaunty swimming trunks;

Send a case of Spanish lace
To a pair of lady skunks.

You could give a fish a dish
For her favorite seaweed stew;

Send three frogs
some sailing togs

And a yachting cap or two.

But **never** tease a weasel.
Now I can't be more precise.
A weasel will not like it —
And teasing
isn't
nice!

You could bake a drake a cake
For his special birthday treat;

You could braid a bug a rug
To make his bug house neat.

You could feed a spider cider
Or perhaps pink lemonade;
Or give a moose some juice
To sip on in the shade.

But **never** tease a weasel.
Now remember what I've said!
It's more fun to please a weasel
And be friends with him instead.

All rights reserved. Published in the United States by Random House Children's Books,
a division of Random House, Inc., New York. Originally published with different illustrations
by Parents' Magazine Press, New York, in 1964.

RANDOM HOUSE and colophon are registered trademarks of Random House, Inc.

www.randomhouse.com/kids

Educators and librarians, for a variety of teaching tools, visit us at
www.randomhouse.com/teachers

Library of Congress Cataloging-in-Publication Data
Soule, Jean Conder.
Never tease a weasel / by Jean Conder Soule ; illustrated by George Booth. — 1st ed.
    p. cm.
SUMMARY: Illustrations and rhyming text present animals in silly situations, such as a pig in
a wig and a moose drinking juice, along with a reminder not to tease.
ISBN 978-0-375-83420-2 (trade) — ISBN 978-0-375-93420-9 (lib. bdg.)
[1. Teasing—Fiction. 2. Animals—Fiction. 3. Humorous stories. 4. Stories in rhyme.]
I. Booth, George, ill. II. Title.
PZ8.3.S715Ne 2007
[E]—dc22
2005023041

PRINTED IN CHINA   10 9 8 7 6 5 4 3   First Edition